PHILO

and the
SUPERHOLIES

written by Mireille Mishriky
illustrated by S. Violette Palumbo

ISBN: 978-1517056018 (Paperback)
ISBN: 978-0-9952459-8-3 (Hardcover)

Published by: Mireille Mishriky, author
www.mireillemishriky.com

Illustrations and book design by S. Violette Palumbo

Printed in the United States of America.
First Printing, 2016

Philo woke up while the sun was still asleep. He could not wait for the day to start. He brushed his teeth but missed a tooth on the right; he was in a great hurry. He washed his face but missed his chin; he wanted to finish quickly. He was going to his friend's birthday party at the park and could not wait for the fun to start.

Philo missed going to the park; he had not been in months. He used to love playing there with his friends. They would ride the swings, go down the slides, and play in the sandbox with their shovels, buckets, and the starfish sieve they all shared. Then, one day, a boy named James moved into the green house next to the park, and the fun stopped.

James loved playing little tricks on everyone at the park. He would spread dirt on the slide just as Philo was going down, pour glue on the shovels, and turn the starfish sieve into a birds' nest. James made Philo and his friends so miserable that they stopped going to the park.

This was why Philo was very excited about his friend's birthday!

The party was at a different park, and James was not invited. Philo and his friends could build sand castles, take turns on the slides, and swing so high they could reach the sky.

It was time to wrap the gift! Philo's grandmother helped him with the ribbon, but he was moving so fast that he kept missing a loop. They had to start over ten times! His grandmother could not understand why he was in such a hurry.

"Grandma, I can't wait to go to the park! I have not been since James moved into the green house," Philo said.

"Philo, you should have activated the SuperHolies to help you deal with James," said Grandma.

"The SuperHolies? What are the SuperHolies?" asked Philo.

"The SuperHolies are the blessings of the Holy Spirit. After baptism, Christians are granted nine SuperHolies. They are superpowers that help Christians make the right choices and overcome obstacles. You received your SuperHolies when you were baptized long ago. You can't see the SuperHolies, but you feel their powers and their influence in your heart," Grandma explained.

Philo was stunned! He had superpowers, and he did not even know about them!

"Grandma, how do I activate the SuperHolies?"

"Just make the sign of the cross, and the SuperHolies will spring into action," answered Grandma.

"Grandma, how can my powers help me?"

"The Peace SuperHoly gives the power to conquer your fears. It reminds you that Jesus is always watching over you and that you should never be afraid."

"Even when it is dark in my room?"

"Yes, dear, especially in darkness,"
 said Grandma.

13

"The Love SuperHoly gives the power to love everyone, just as Jesus loves us all."

14

"The Joy SuperHoly gives the power to feel happy all the time, even in sad situations."

"Like the day I broke my bike?"

"Exactly!" said Grandma.

15

"The Kindness SuperHoly gives the power to remain sweet when others are mean and to become friends with people who are difficult to get along with."

"The Patience SuperHoly gives the power to wait when you want something right away, like eating an ice cream or going to your friend's birthday party."

"I could use this power today!"
said Philo, chuckling.

17

"The Goodness SuperHoly gives you the power to say no to bad choices and to speak the truth when you think lying would get you out of trouble."

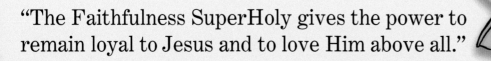
"The Faithfulness SuperHoly gives the power to remain loyal to Jesus and to love Him above all."

"The Gentleness SuperHoly gives the power to treat everyone with tenderness and to speak kindly."

"The Self-Control SuperHoly gives the power to control your actions and to manage your feelings and anger."

"Even when my cousins make a mess in my room?"

"Yes, even then!"

21

"When the SuperHolies are strengthened through prayers and communion, Christians are capable of amazing things," said Grandma.

"My superpowers are awesome, Grandma!"

"So you should not worry about James."

"I am not worried; he won't be at the park."

"Philo, you should never worry because you have the SuperHolies. Just make the sign of the cross to activate them, and they will help you when you are in need."

"Thanks, Grandma! I am off to the party. See you at dinnertime!"

Philo arrived at the party and was stunned to see James at the park. James was running around, popping the balloons, and making everyone feel miserable.

"Hi, Philo! Are you going to go down the slide now?" asked James with a grin.

Philo knew what James meant; he was going to spread dirt on the slide!

Suddenly, Philo remembered his grandmother's advice. He made the sign of the cross to activate the SuperHolies.

The SuperHolies sprang into action. After a brief discussion, they agreed that the Kindness SuperHoly was the best power to help Philo deal with James.

"What if James just wanted to become your friend but did not know how to ask?" whispered the Kindness SuperHoly.

"What if James was trying to make you and your friends laugh so you would invite him to play with you? Maybe he was lonely and was trying to grab your attention. Sure, he played awful tricks on you and your friends, but Jesus taught us to forgive."

Philo could not see the Kindness SuperHoly, but he suddenly felt sorry for James and believed that he should at least give him a chance.

"James, would you like to play with us?"

The other children were shocked! No one had ever invited James to join in the fun before.

James was thrilled! He gave Philo such a big hug that he lifted him off the ground.

"No more tricks?" asked Philo.

"I promise. I just wanted someone to play with!" said James.

The birthday party was loads of fun, and James was very nice throughout.

Grandma was right; Christians have awesome superpowers.

Which SuperHoly will Philo activate next?

Dear reader,

I hope that you enjoyed the story of Philo and the SuperHolies.

I pray that the story inspires you to activate your SuperHolies, especially during challenging moments.

I would love to hear from you! Let me know which SuperHoly is your favorite.

You can send me a note at author@mireillemishriky.com or visit with me on the web at www.mireillemishriky.com or https://www.facebook.com/Mireillemishrikyauthor/

Finally, I would like to ask you a favor. If you are so inclined, I would love to have you write a review of Philo and the SuperHolies. Just post your review on Amazon or any other online bookstore you frequent. I am eager to hear your feedback on this story.

Thank you so much for reading Philo and the SuperHolies and spending time with me.

God Bless,

Mireille

P.S. If you have enjoyed this story, you might also like Philo and the Patience SuperHoly (volume 2).

Made in the USA
Middletown, DE
03 January 2021